THE CAKE

Dorothée de Monfreid

THE CAKE

GECKO PRESS

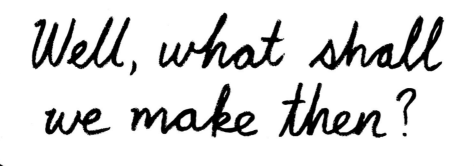

This edition first published in 2014 by Gecko Press
PO Box 9335, Marion Square, Wellington 6141, New Zealand
info@geckopress.com

English language edition © Gecko Press Ltd 2014

First American edition published in 2014 by Gecko Press USA, an imprint of Gecko Press Ltd.
A catalog record for this book is available from the US Library of Congress.

Distributed in the United States and Canada by Lerner Publishing Group, www.lernerbooks.com
Distributed in the United Kingdom by Bounce Sales and Marketing, www.bouncemarketing.co.uk
Distributed in Australia by Scholastic Australia, www.scholastic.com.au
Distributed in New Zealand by Random House NZ, www.randomhouse.co.nz

A catalogue record for this book is available from the National Library of New Zealand.

Original title: *Le gâteau*
Text and illustrations by Dorothée de Monfreid
© 2001 l'école des loisirs, Paris

Translated by Linda Burgess
Edited by Penelope Todd
Typesetting by Vida & Luke Kelly, New Zealand
Printed in China by Everbest Printing Co Ltd, an accredited ISO 14001 & FSC certified printer

Hardback ISBN: 978-1-877579-45-5
Paperback ISBN: 978-1-927271-44-5

For more curiously good books, visit www.geckopress.com